BY PETER LIPPMAN

The KNOW-IT-ALLS Take a Winter Vacation

Doubleday & Company, Inc., Garden City, New York

Library of Congress Catalog Card Number 81-43433
Library of Congress Cataloging in Publication Data
Lippman, Peter J.   The Know-It-Alls take a winter vacation.
  Summary: The Know-It-Alls pursue their favorite winter sports while misadventure pursues them.
  [1. Alligators—Fiction. 2. Winter sports—Fiction. 3. Vacations—Fiction] I. Title.
PZ7.L666Kp [E] 81-43433 AACR2
ISBN: 0-385-17398-9   Copyright © 1982 by Peter Lippman

As soon as the Know-It-Alls arrived at the resort for their winter vacation, Annie, Ernest and Mother helped Father Know-It-All out onto the ice skating rink.

While Mother, Annie and Ernest signed up for the different events, Father bellowed out to the other skaters, "Follow me! I'll show you what I learned in the skating lessons I took twenty years ago. O.K., everybody, for the first lesson, leg up and we do a spiral."

"Second, a jump,

third, a spin,

fourth, everyone in line for speed skating,

and fifth, a turn and hockey stop.''

All the skaters did a neat turn and stop except Father Know-It-All. "Oops, that was the lesson I missed," he said as he plowed into the others.

Mother Know-It-All had just snowshoed to the top of a mountain when a huge bear jumped out of a hole and grabbed her. "Take my picture or else," he roared.

"Step back," she replied, "or the picture won't come out."

Following orders, the bear stepped back and fell over the cliff into a snow bank. Mother yelled to him, "It's O.K. I got some great shots, and I'll send you a few prints as soon as the rangers give me your new address."

Annie joined a bobsled team. "I'll steer," she said.

Off they went. When they came to a
fork in the trail, everyone said,
"Right, right!"
"No, no," said Annie,
"I know left is right."

They left the bobsled trail, headed down the hotel driveway, shot in the back door, flew through the kitchen, past the cook, into the dining room, onto the table, and . . .

. . . most of the team finished the race in the soup except Annie, who landed in the maître d's lap. "The soup is very good," she told him, "but it needs a little more salt."

At the lake, an ice fisherman offered to show Ernest how to cut a hole in the ice. "No, no. I've got a better way so that you can saw a perfect circle," said Ernest.

"Really?" said the fisherman.

"Just do as I say," said Ernest. "First you stand in the center and then keep turning as you saw.

There! It's a perfect circle," he said as the fisherman sank down into the water.

Ernest helped thaw him out. In spite of everything, the fisherman was quite happy because he and Ernest had caught the biggest fish.

Then everyone joined in for the grand finale of the great Snow Carnival—the Giant Ski Race and Snow Sculpture Contest.

At first the Know-It-Alls were a little behind the other skiers. Father didn't see the tree because he was telling Mother Know-It-All how to ski.

Mother Know-It-All tripped over Father Know-It-All because she was telling Annie how to ski, who was telling Ernest how to ski, who was reading a how-to-ski book.

The Know-It-Alls started rolling down the
mountain. They became one big snowball.

They whizzed by all the other skiers down the ski jump, past the finish line and . . .

Back home the Know-It-Alls had a pool party. They showed their friends and neighbors their trophies and told them how to skate, bobsled, photograph bears, ice fish and make snow sculpture. Then everybody signed their names on Ernest's cast.